KT-497-229

THIS BOOK
BELONGS TO

THE FLINTSTONES™ 1991 ANNUAL is published by Marvel Comics Ltd, 13/15 Arundel Street, London WC2. THE FLINTSTONES is a trademark of Hanna-Barbera Productions Inc. Copyright © 1968/1969/1990 Hanna-Barbera Productions Inc. All rights reserved. Printed in Italy.

CONTENTS

COMIC STRIPS

Flintstone – Mega-Movie Star 6
Feeling Ill, Getting Better 24
Weight-Up 54

PUZZLES AND GAMES

Carved Code 14
Babysitting Blunders 18
2 Minute Maze 23
Find the Twins 40
Make a Dino-Dynamo 45
Dino's Din-Dins 46
Fix-up the Mix-up 51
Dinosaur Derby 52

STORIES

Dino's Midnight Walk 15
Car Wash Capers 20
Stoneage Pursuit 41
The Masked Bowler 48

8

9

10

11

12

DINO'S MIDNIGHT WALK

A late-night walk for Dino brings trouble for Fred!

It had been a tough week at the Quarry. A rush order for large stones had come through from a group calling itself the Stonehenge Society, so Fred had been working long hours of overtime.

"I'm dog-tired," he sighed, flopping into his favourite armchair after a late supper.

"Glad you're not dinosaur-tired," smiled Wilma. "Dino needs his last walk."

Fred groaned and struggled out of his chair. "Walkies, Din-oooh!" he said as the faithful pet leapt at Fred on hearing the magic words.

Outside it was a warm, crystal-clear night, with a gleaming moon and shimmering, sparkling stars. Fred yawned. "We ain't goin' far, Dino," he warned sleepily, though Dino, trotting on purposefully, seemed to know different.

Moments later, his nose twitched and his head jerked up as he heard something suspicious over at the cave home they were passing. Fred, whose nose didn't twitch and whose head didn't jerk up, heard nothing. He'd have carried on, practically sleep walking, had Dino not suddenly charged across the front garden, dragging Fred, on the lead, behind him.

"Dino, stop!" Fred protested as he was pulled across the lawn on his stomach. His pet dinosaur paid no attention, stampeding on and hauling Fred after him. Fred couldn't see why Dino had bolted – in fact he could see very little, he discovered, when being dragged along at speed on ground level. Something solid and hard began to loom towards him however – something very like a garden wall.

With one graceful leap, Dino jumped over the wall and Fred ploughed straight into it. **BASH!**

Fred found himself on the neighbouring lawn with loose stones littered around him. For the first time that night he noticed shimmering, sparkling stars, though they were hard to miss now, as they danced right before his eyes. Fred also noticed that Dino was nowhere to be seen.

Fred crept through gardens looking for Dino. He couldn't even holler, **"DIIIINOOO!"** at the top of his voice because he'd wake half of Bedrock doing that, so he settled for hissing his pet's name instead. It was all useless – Dino had disappeared and the exhausted Fred felt like giving up the search.

"See what I see?" whispered one cop to another, as Fred prowled through the garden in front of their car.

"Looks like our guy," the cop's partner answered, and hit the flint switch which brought their glow-worm headlights to life.

Suddenly bathed in light, Fred stopped dead in his tracks. "Freeze!" ordered the first cop unnecessarily as they dashed from their car. An instant later he thumped one hand hard on Fred's shoulder, almost knocking the wind out of him. "Lefty Livingstone I presume!" the cop added. "The burglar who's been terrorising the neighbourhood for weeks, caught red-handed!"

"Hey, wait a second," blurted Fred. "I'm not this Livingstone guy, I'm no burglar."

"Yeah, yeah," answered the second cop. "You can tell our nice Sergeant Granite all about it – down at the station!"

At Bedrock police headquarters, Sergeant Granite remained stony-faced as Fred outlined what had happened. Fred could see Granite didn't believe him, and when he learned

"Gee, it's – it's come to this," the man began. "Here am – ooh – I, Lefty Livingstone, finest burglar in Bedrock, needing help from – ooch – the cops." Everyone's mouths dropped open – the police officers were amazed, and Fred was yawning again. "I'm – arrh – giving myself up," the troubled Lefty continued, "because maybe – ooh – you guys can get it off me . . ." He struggled further into the station. Something was with him. Something which had its teeth sunk into Lefty's bottom. Something which looked like Dino.

"It started – ooh – chasing me as I finished another job . . ."

"And, er, he's been on your tail, so to speak, ever since," chuckled Fred. "That's my boy! That's my Dino!"

Dino looked up and saw Fred for the first time. To Lefty's relief, he let go of the burglar, bounded over to Fred and began a face-licking frenzy. "Cut it out! Cut it out!" laughed Fred.

"Seems, sir, we owe you an apology – and our gratitude," Sergeant Granite said.

After making a statement and chiselling his name to it, Fred and Dino went home. Dawn had already broken, but Fred went straight to bed. Just as he was climbing in, the alarm went off.

"I don't believe it," he moaned, "it's time for work again!"

"Work?" asked Wilma sleepily. "On a Saturday?"

Fred was so tired he'd forgotten he could have a lie-in that morning. "Yabba-ahhhr-Dabba-ahhhr-Dmmmph . . ." he yawned as his head finally hit the pillow.

two burglaries had been reported at caves close to where he'd been arrested, Fred feared the worst. He comforted himself with the thought that the cell would at least have a bed. He was almost looking forward to being locked up and getting some sleep when a man wearing a burglar's mask popped his head around a wall.

BABYSITTING BLUNDERS

Fred is grumpy after a few days of bad luck. To prove he can do something right he has volunteered to babysit Pebbles and Bamm-Bamm while the others go shopping. If he appears to have survived the day without any disasters,

18

Wilma has promised him a **SPECIAL TREAT!**

TO PLAY THE GAME:– You will need a dice, a counter per player and a **SPECIAL TREAT** for the winner (eg. sweets or cake).
The player who scores highest with the dice and avoids most of Fred's disasters will win the **PRIZE** which should be placed on the **FINISH** zone!

CAR WASH CAPERS

With Wilma away, Fred has a bright idea for cleaning the dishes.

"Relax, Barney! I've got it all figured out!"

Barney had heard his neighbour say these words many times. They usually meant trouble.

"You've got lots to clean up, Fred," warned Barney. "And Wilma, Betty and the kids are back from their weekend at Wilma's folks in a couple of hours."

"It's all under control, Barn," Fred insisted. He had his feet up on the kitchen table, and was thumbing through the Sunday paper. Behind him, the mound of used pans and dishes piled high in the sink and through the window, Barney could see Fred's grime-stained car, and Dino rolling in the garden mud. Barney wondered what Fred's idea of out of control was.

"The best part is, little buddy, I hardly have to do anything! C'mon, I'll show you . . ."

Fred drove Barney, Dino, the soiled dishes, a box of washing powder and a carton of dinosaur shampoo to a brand new motor garage service station close to Bedrock river. A sign pointing to one

conveyor belt. The driver inserted a coin in a box by the wheel. Immediately, a large juicy steak dropped down from the box and dangled tantalisingly before the dinosaur. He jumped up and ran for the steak. The dinosaur couldn't reach it because he was in the wheel, but as he ran, the wheel turned, and so did the roller on the conveyor belt.

side said: **Automatic Car Wash.** Barney looked puzzled. "Watch," said Fred, "there's a car about to go through."

Barney stared as the driver parked his vehicle on a long conveyor belt. He walked over to a dinosaur seated in a giant exercise wheel. The hub of the wheel, Barney noted, was connected to the end roller of the

"Neat, huh?" grinned Fred. "Now, the car is moving to that first pair of woolly mammoths on either side of the belt."

The mammoths squirted Bedrock river water from their trunks at the car. Then as the conveyor belt moved the car on, its roof bumped into a container dangling above. This tipped up, and washing powder

tumbled onto the car, frothing and bubbling as it mixed with the water.

"Hey, the car's getting washed!" Barney chuckled.

"The rinse comes next," added Fred. "Watch the second pair of mammoths." These, like the first pair, were either side of the belt. They also squirted water from their trunks as the car past them, rinsing off the soap suds.

Now keep an eye on the steak," Fred said. The meat was wound back into its box, but reappeared moments later on the other side of the wheel. The dinosaur turned, then started running in the opposite direction after the steak again. The wheel turned once more, causing the conveyor to reverse, bringing the car back towards the mammoths. Barney saw that the woolly creatures had also turned and had their backs to the belt this time, which meant the car was pulled between their thick coats.

"The front pair dry the car off," Fred pointed out, "and the second pair buff it up to a nice shine."

"Gee, Fred," sighed Barney, "modern technology is amazin'!"

"Right!" agreed Fred, wandering back to his own car. "And I'm going to use it to maximum advantage."

Barney watched Fred sprinkle lots of washing powder over the dirty dishes, then squeeze dinosaur shampoo on Dino. "Get the picture, Barn?" he asked.

But as Fred finished, an attendant hung up an Out Of Order sign on the car wash. "Sorry, fellas," he called over, "but our 'saur's ran his quota

of miles for today."

"Looks like you're all washed up, Fred," joked Barney, but Fred wasn't laughing. He groaned and slumped heavily against the back of his car. Unfortunately the hand brake wasn't on, and it rolled forward. Fred fell flat as it moved away and on towards the river. He howled in despair as his car, plus dishes and dinosaur, rolled into the water, then under it.

Dino's head popped up to mark where the car had settled. The garage attendant loaned Fred a tow truck and after swimming out to attach a line, he was able to haul the car back to dry land. Soaking wet, like his car, his crockery, and his pet, Fred drove home.

There, Wilma was waiting and Fred sheepishly climbed out of the car. "Fred, I'm proud of you!" Wilma beamed, however. "You've got Dino and the car spotless – but, er, why have you been driving around with clean dishes . . .?"

"Huh?" Fred gasped. Then he realised that everything was covered in washing powder when the car went into the river. It all came out clean, then dried off on the journey home. "Well, er, they were damp, so I took 'em for a spin. Spin drying – geddit?" he joked. He was relieved when Wilma laughed and went inside.

"Narrow escape," whispered Barney.

"Gimme a break, Barn," grinned Fred. "Everything's spick and span, and I didn't even have to pay for the car wash. I really cleaned up . . .!"

2 MINUTE MAZE

Fred has two minutes to get to work. If he is late again his boss, Mr Slate, will give him the sack! Time yourself and see if you can help Fred to complete the maze in two minutes.

OFFICE

PHEEEP!

SLATES QUARRY

26

29

30

31

32

33

34

35

37

38

FIND THE TWINS

Help Pebbles and Bamm-Bamm to find the two baby twin dinosaurs which are exactly alike.

40

Fred Flintstone, a master of that well-known general knowledge game, Stoneage Pursuit, appears on a television game show!

"Okay, pink it is – entertainment, Fred," said Barney.

"Fire away," grinned Fred confidently.

"Who were the stars of the movie, *BrontoCop*?"

"Easy – Dash Riprock, and Roxy La Block. Correct?"

"I told you he'd know it, Betty," sighed Wilma. "Trust my husband to be a complete genius at something as useless as *Stoneage Pursuit!*"

"It needn't be useless," Betty said as she began to pack away the bone dice and the ivory-playing pieces. "You can win lots of money and big prizes on the tv version of *Stoneage Pursuit*. You should enter, Fred – you might clean up . . ."

That was all the encouragement Fred needed. The next day he applied to go on the show – a programme he had often watched with a tv dinner of stegosaurus stew on his lap. Between mouthfuls, he would shout out the answers, usually quicker than the contestants taking part. Once, in his excitement, he had forgotten he wasn't between mouthfuls and had had to spend the rest of the programme cleaning the television screen. Though he enjoyed the show, he had never really thought about going on it himself until Betty had mentioned it, but in the days that followed, he thought of little else. When an invitation to appear on the show arrived, he was over the moon.

41

"This is it, Wilma — a chance to win and win big!" enthused Fred as he and Wilma waited for the show to begin. "The top prize tonight is a fortnight's holiday in Rockapulco!"

"I know, Fred," Wilma replied, "but to win that you have to gamble with all the other prizes you've won along the way. If you get that far, you'll have done really well, so play safe and don't gamble, huh?"

Fred didn't have time to answer as just then he was called onto the set. He was very nervous, and felt like there were pterodactyls fluttering in his stomach when he heard the title music playing. The host, Rex Tyrannosaurus, was always grinning in a smile that displayed more teeth in one mouth than Fred had ever seen, but he quickly put Fred and the other contestants at ease.

In the first round, Fred answered several questions correctly and began to relax, particularly when he won bonus prizes of his and hers granite-faced fashion watches **and** a colour television set. His cash total was the highest after the first round, so he easily qualified for round two.

"In this round," Rex explained for the viewers at home, "our two finalists buzz to answer a question. So, take up your positions, contestants, and test those buzzards!"

Fred and the other contestant, a short, jolly-looking man named Sidney Shale, moved behind two desks, each with a bird upon it. Sidney pressed his bird's head, and the creature went **"Meeep!"** Fred tried his bird's head, and it went **"Arrrk!"**

"Great," Rex enthused, "both buzzards are working so on with the show!

"Art and literature — who wrote

Alice In Dinosaur Land?"

"**Arrrk!**" went Fred's buzzard. "Lewis Fossil!" answered Fred.

"Right!" said Rex. "Now – sport and leisure. Who plays at Rocks Stadium?"

"Meeep!" Sidney this time. "The Pittsburgh Stoners?"

"Sorry, Sidney," replied Rex. "Fred, can you take it . . .?"

"The Buffalo Boulders," Fred answered correctly. He began to feel really confident . . .

Barney and Betty were watching at home, babysitting Pebbles.

"Gee, Fred's doing great," smiled Barney. "He's just won another bonus prize."

"Yes, Wilma's wanted a bone china coffee set made of real bone for a long time," agreed Betty. "It looks like Fred's going to win easily, but will he decide to gamble all he's won against the star prize . . .?"

". . . And tonight's final question is on science and nature. Which now extinct creature is generally agreed to have been the ugliest, most hideous beast on Earth?"

"**Arrrk!**" went Fred's bird for the umpteenth time. "The Eyesaur!" answered Fred triumphantly. He was right again, to finish as one of the biggest winners ever on _Stoneage Pursuit!_ Sidney Shale warmly congratulated him, as did question master Rex, who brought Fred forward for the Star Prize Challenge.

Fred surveyed the prizes he'd already won, and remembered Wilma's warning about playing safe. Yet he felt so confident that when Rex asked if he wanted to try the Star Prize question, risking all he'd won on a wrong answer, Fred decided to go for it.

"Now, Fred," Rex began, "Spin the category wheel, then I'll ask you a question on the subject it pinpoints. You have just fifteen seconds to answer, and I must accept the first answer you give me." Fred nodded, and span the wheel. It came to rest with the needle pointing at entertainment – Fred's favourite topic. He felt really confident now.

"Here we go," said Rex, building the excitement. "Tonight's Star Prize question on entertainment is . . . Who were the stars of the movie *BrontoCop?*"

Fred couldn't believe his ears. It was the same question he'd had just the other night. He couldn't contain himself, and burst out laughing – it was all going to be too easy for words. Fred continued to roar with laughter as the seconds ticked by. Wilma held her breath in the wings. Rex looked confused, but kept one eye on the clock. "Have to hurry you, Fred," he warned.

When he saw there were just three seconds left, Fred quickly

suppressed his giggles and answered without thinking. "Dash La Block and Roxy Riprock," he said. Then, "No, wait – I mean . . ."

"Sorry, Fred," Rex began sombrely, "but I have to take your first answer which, as you know, isn't correct."

Fred smiled bravely for the rest of the show, but when the theme tune came on, he trudged dejectedly away to where Wilma was waiting. "I blew it, Wilma," he mumbled sadly. "I should have listened to you, but I guess I just got over-confident out there. We've still got the money I won, but we should have had so much more – can you ever forgive me?"

"Oh Fred," Wilma smiled, putting her arms around her husband's neck, "surely a quiz-master like you knows the answer to that one." She planted a big kiss on his lips.

"I guess I Yabba-Dabba-**Doo!**" said Fred, starting to laugh again.

YOU WILL NEED:– A sheet of thin card, some tracing paper, a pair of scissors, a paper fastener, a pencil and something to colour with.

1. Draw around Dino's body and leg shapes on your tracing paper. Carefully cut out these shapes.
2. Place the two shapes on your card and draw around them, marking the position of the holes.
3. Cut out the shapes from your card and pierce holes in positions marked.*
4. Draw and colour Dino's features on each section.
5. Fasten the legs section to the rear of the body section (as shown). Check that the legs move freely and that the paper fastener is not too tight. Spin the legs and watch your Dino-Dynamo dash!

*IMPORTANT: Ask an adult to help you with this.

DINO'S DIN-DINS

Pebbles and Bamm-Bamm love to feed Dino his favourite Bronto-Burgers. Follow the instructions to make a game in which you too can feed Dino.

TO MAKE THE GAME YOU WILL NEED:— A large cardboard box, two or three margarine tub type lids, a pair of scissors, some paper, sellotape and something to draw and colour with.

IMPORTANT: Ask an adult to help you with this.

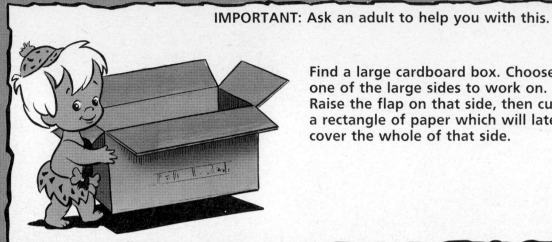

Find a large cardboard box. Choose one of the large sides to work on. Raise the flap on that side, then cut a rectangle of paper which will later cover the whole of that side.

Draw a grid of squares on this paper and copy the wide-mouthed picture of Dino as shown.* Colour the picture and tape it to the side of your box.

*Make certain that Dino's mouth is wider than your tub lids!

Carefully pierce the line around Dino's mouth repeatedly with a pencil point until you can push the inner area through into the box. Support the picture side box flap by taping it to the two adjacent raised flaps.

Now that you've made a 'Hungry Dino', you have to make his food –
BRONTO BURGER FRISBEES!

Find any circular margarine tub type lids. Ensure that Dino's mouth is big enough for the lids to pass through comfortably.
Place the lids on a sheet of paper and draw around them. Cut out the circles.

Draw pictures (as shown) of BRONTO-BURGERS on each of your circles. Tape the pictures to the margarine lids.

Each player must stand at an agreed distance from Dino and throw BRONTO-BURGERS frisbee style into Dino's mouth.

The player who feeds Dino the most burgers after ten throws wins the game!

"Don't be long, Fred," Wilma called after her husband, "Pebbles and Bamm-Bamm want their ice-cream."

"Me too," chuckled Fred, running off to get the treats. "Back in a flash."

Wilma and Fred were with Betty, Barney and the kids on a picnic in Bedrock Park. They sat on a grassy slope overlooking the lake, watching several people messing about in giant turtle shells on the water.

"Help, Help!" one of them suddenly called out. "Our turtle shell's sprung a leak, and we can't swim!"

"Those people are in trouble!" said Barney anxiously. A second later, there was a blinding flash, and a figure seemed to appear from nowhere at the lakeside. He wore a tiger-skin cape, and a white mask which covered his face, save for his eyes and mouth. In his hands was a large, white bowling ball, which had a length of twine attached to it.

"The Masked Bowler, Bedrock's own super-hero," Barney gasped. The Bowler took aim, then sent his bowling ball skimming across the water towards the people in the sinking turtle shell. They grabbed the ball and hung on as the hero pulled in the twine hauling them to safety. There was another dazzling flash, and the Masked Bowler mysteriously vanished again.

"Wow, what a guy!" cooed Betty.

"He's the best," enthused Barney. "It's a shame Fred missed it."

Fred returned later with the ice-creams, and they told him about the rescue. "You didn't see him foil those crooks at the supermarket either," said Wilma. "You were parking the car while I saw the whole thing."

"Yes, you missed him at the quarry, too, when we had that cave-in," Barney added. "He rolled his

**ASKED
LER**

special bowling ball into the rocks to make an escape route for the trapped workers."

"Hey," Betty frowned suspiciously, "How come Fred's always missing whenever the Masked Bowler appears . . .?"

Betty, Barney and Wilma gazed in amazement at Fred. "What? What is it?" he asked. Beside him, unseen by anyone, Pebbles had torn some holes in a paper napkin. She stood up, and stretched the napkin across Fred's face so that his eyes and mouth showed through the holes.

"The Masked Bowler!" everyone shouted.

That was the end of their quiet picnic. It seemed as though everyone in the park had crowded over to meet Bedrock's hero. The clamour continued the following day, when the newspaper reporters and tv crew came to the Flintstones' house. Fred was suddenly the most popular guy in town. He was a celebrity, he was famous, and he couldn't help but enjoy it. Fred thought that it was very nice to be famous, but there was just one tiny detail that bothered him. Fred wasn't the Masked Bowler after all.

Several days of presents, free dinners, and general hero worship later, Fred – 'the un-Masked Bowler' as he'd become known – was invited to receive the Freedom of Bedrock by the mayor. Fred had tried to say, "Er, sorry, but I'm not actually the Masked Bowler as such . . ." He really did try extra hard to say it again when the mayor gave him the award, though the words that came out were, "Thank-you so much for this great honour."

The ceremony was interrupted, however, when a policeman rushed onto the platform. He informed everyone that a deadly man-eating dinosaur had climbed inside a down-town office block. "Sounds like a job for the Masked Bowler!" the mayor

announced. Fred agreed, then realised that meant he had to tackle the savage 'saur.

"Nothing is impossible until you try," Fred told himself as he stood, shaking, before the snarling creature in the office block. A large crowd waited silently outside. Fred's hands were sweating so much, he could barely hold his bowling ball. Nevertheless, he wound himself up, and hurtled the ball at the dinosaur. It bounced off the creature, having no effect except to make it roar even more ferociously. Fred had another go, and another, and another for good luck – of which there was none as the creature remained unmoved. "Well, you tried," Fred told himself, "and it was impossible."

Suddenly, a shining white bowling ball whistled past Fred's ear and clattered into the dinosaur, rendering it senseless and harmless. Fred turned to see a man in a tiger-skinned cape and white mask behind him. "The Masked Bowler, at your service," the man said.

"Boy am I glad to see you," Fred grinned.

"Sure I won't cramp your style?" the Bowler asked. "You seem to have enjoyed being me just recently."

Fred blushed. He began explaining how the adulation had swept him along, how he couldn't put a stop to it even when he tried. "That's the problem with fame," the hero remarked wisely, "it's why I keep my true identity secret. You'll have to tell that crowd out there the truth, but I'll help. I wouldn't be a hero otherwise, would I?"

Fred bravely confessed to the crowd. The Masked Bowler then appeared, telling them that he was grateful to Fred for doing heroic work in softening up the dinosaur, and in the end, everyone forgave Fred.

Wilma was especially pleased when he came home as just ordinary Fred Flintstone. She hadn't fancied the idea of having to wash clean a tiger-skin cape and white mask one little bit . . .!

Fix-up the mix-up

WHOOPS! This story has been jumbled up. Can you tell which order the pictures should go in?

DINOSAUR

THIS GAME IS FOR TWO TO FOUR PLAYERS. YOU NEED A DICE AND ONE COUNTER FOR EACH PLAYER.

HEAVY GROUND GO BACK 3 PLACES.

YOU'RE FEELING STRONG! 1 EXTRA THROW!

FIN

YABBA DA

Players must complete one lap of the board before they enter the *home straight*. Players must throw the exact number with their dice to land their counter on the finish area. . .

YOU STUMBLE ON SOFT TURF GO BACK 4 PLACES.

52

REFUSE TO JUMP FENCE. MISS A THROW.

DERBY

Each player must choose a jockey and place their counter on that area. Throw a six to begin to move clockwise.

ISH

BA DOO!

THIRSTY! STOP TO DRINK AT THE WATER JUMP. GO BACK 4.

. . . if they don't they must return along the home straight the appropriate number of places and wait to throw again.

EGGED ON BY THE CHEERING CROWD. 1 EXTRA THROW.

55

56

58

59